Four Winds Press · New York

Going to Moscow
and other stories

written and illustrated by Arnold Dobrin

PUBLISHED BY FOUR WINDS PRESS.

A DIVISION OF SCHOLASTIC MAGAZINES, INC., NEW YORK, N.Y.

COPYRIGHT © 1973 BY ARNOLD DOBRIN.

ALL RIGHTS RESERVED.

PRINTED IN THE UNITED STATES OF AMERICA.

LIBRARY OF CONGRESS CATALOGUE CARD NUMBER: 73-76457

contents

*A coachful of travelers going to Moscow
discover that things are often not what they seem.*

Going to Moscow

The horses pranced and reared, eager to be off on the journey. Dogs barked and a baby cried. People gave orders to have their luggage strapped to the top of the carriage and climbed inside. There was an old woman, a young man and a mother with her baby and two young children.

When everyone was comfortably seated the driver climbed to his box on the top of the carriage. He had just taken the reins in his hands when suddenly a little old man hobbled toward the carriage, half-running and half-walking, "Wait! Wait!" he shouted excitedly.

8

As he hurriedly ran up to the carriage, the old man kept his hands stiffly in front of himself with his two short thumbs sticking straight up. From the crook of one arm a small traveling bag dangled but otherwise the man seemed to have no luggage.

When he saw that he had another passenger the driver grumbled, put down the reins and climbed down from his box. "Where are you hurrying to, grandfather?" he asked.

"All the way to Moscow," said the old man. "How much is the fare?"

When the driver told him that it was three kopecks the old man still kept his hands stiffly in front of him and asked the driver to take the right amount of money from the little traveling bag that hung from his arm.

As the driver fumbled with the bag, the people inside the carriage watched what was happening. The old woman shook her head from side to side as she said, "What a terrible thing. The poor man can't move his hands!"

"It certainly is a pity," the young mother agreed.

10

Then the young man said, "Life can be hard all right! My grandmother can't even walk."

The coachman gently helped the paralyzed man into the coach while the mother took her baby on her lap to make more room for him. Everybody was quiet as they watched the sad scene of the man who couldn't move his hands or thumbs.

The coachman pulled the reins, cracked his whip and the carriage was off, dashing through the lovely countryside. It was a beautiful sunny day in spring and the meadows were full of flowers. Near the sparkling streams, young shepherds tended their flocks of goats. Girls were feeding chickens in the courtyards of prosperous farms and nature seemed joyous and happy.

But inside the carriage the travelers were silent as they watched the sad little old man. He sat perfectly still, never moving, his hands and thumbs always in front of him.

When the carriage stopped at an inn, the young man said thoughtfully, "Here grandfather, let me help you down." He carefully guided the old man into the inn where the ladies had ordered tea and cakes.

Without even asking if the old man wanted tea, the old woman held a cup to his lips and tucked a napkin in his lap. From time to time the little girl fed him a piece of sweet plum cake which he seemed to enjoy greatly.

In fact, the old man appeared to be enjoying the entire experience and was very grateful for everyone's help. "Thank you," he said, "thank you so very much. You are all extremely kind people. And do not think I will easily forget such kindness."

Even the little boy wanted to be of help. With his own money he ran out to the front desk where he bought a paper and then he held it in front of the old man so that he could read. The child turned the pages carefully whenever the poor old fellow nodded to show that he was finished.

The little boy's arms began to hurt terribly but he was brave and kept on holding the paper up as long as he could.

Meanwhile, in other parts of the inn, people gossiped and clicked their tongues at the sad scene.

14

After they had rested and eaten, the passengers climbed back into the carriage. The driver got back on his box and cracked his whip in the air. He never used it on the horses for he too was a kindly man. He watched the horses struggling to pull the carriage up a steep hill and thought of the paralyzed old man inside. "Ah, it is true," he thought, "everyone has some sadness to bear in this life."

After their tea and cakes everyone felt a little sleepy and began to doze in their corners of the carriage. Only the old man kept his eyes wide open and his hands in front of him.

16

Soon they came to a village where the young man left the carriage and went his way. A half hour passed, the carriage came to another village and the old woman said goodbye and went toward her home.

Finally there were just the young mother, her young children and the old man left in the carriage. Already she could see some of the buildings of Moscow coming into view. But most of the time she was busy trying to hush her little boy and girl who were busy whispering in a corner of the carriage. They knew they would soon arrive in the center of the city and that the little old man would be going on his way. Finally, they could no longer control their curiosity.

17

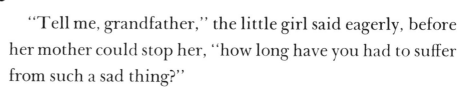

"Tell me, grandfather," the little girl said eagerly, before her mother could stop her, "how long have you had to suffer from such a sad thing?"

"What sad thing?" asked the little old man.

"Why — your hands," the girl said, "your paralyzed hands."

The old man raised his eyebrows and looked down at his hands.

"Oh my dear child," he explained, "this isn't paralysis— it is just a measurement. Since I was going to Moscow my wife asked me to buy her a pair of shoes. I measured her feet carefully and this is the exact length — the distance between my two thumbs. Her shoes must be exactly right — neither too large or too small. You don't know my wife! She would have a terrible temper tantrum if I got the wrong size!"

18

The story of a clever boy
who outwits a greedy woman.

FAT OLGA

Fat Olga was not a very nice woman. She yelled at children, she ordered her husband around and was not kind to animals. Olga was greedy too. The thing that she liked most of all was to trick another person out of something that she wanted.

Olga was so clever that all of the villagers learned to be very careful when they had any dealings with her. Even beyond the village, Olga was known as a sharp-eyed, sharp-tongued woman who had a way of getting her hands on things before anybody knew what was happening.

At the marketplace she always demanded the freshest meat and fish. But her own customers could never be sure of what they were getting. "Beware when you buy fruit from Olga!" they told strangers in the town. "It's pretty on top but underneath—*garbage*!"

23

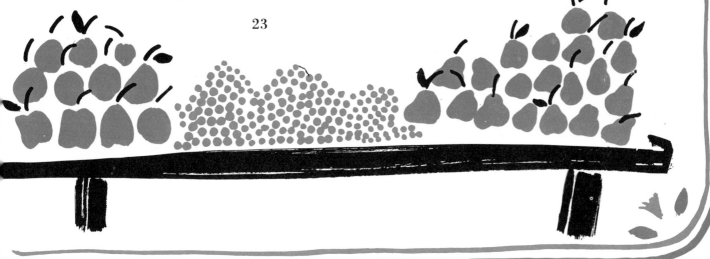

Like all greedy people, Fat Olga was always looking around for an opportunity or a person who she could use to her own advantage. The older villagers knew her so well that few of them were ever tricked by the old woman. But occasionally a young person would fall into her traps. And when he did, he usually found himself a little poorer.

For a long time Olga had been keeping her eye on Grisha, a poor boy who lived alone on a small farm not far from the village. His parents were so poor when they died that they left their son nothing but the farm and a fine goat.

One day as she sat behind her fruit stand Olga heard Grisha asking for advice from the fish lady, a kindly soul who managed everyone's lives.

25

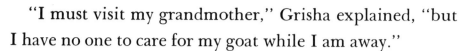

"I must visit my grandmother," Grisha explained, "but I have no one to care for my goat while I am away."

The fish lady answered "Don't worry Grisha! You have a good goat and someone will be glad to care for her. I will ask *all* of my friends. Just don't have a worry!"

But already Fat Olga had quickly hatched a plan.

"Leave your goat with me," she said as she waddled over to Grisha. "I will make cheese from the milk and half I will give to you when you return. And it will be delicious—I promise you that!"

The fish lady looked very worried. She just began to say, "But Grisha—I know of someone else you—" when Grisha sputtered, "What a fair offer! I accept with thanks!"

Grisha was away two weeks. When he came back, tired and weary, he looked forward to taking his goat home. He wanted to drink her milk and to eat the good cheese that Fat Olga had promised him. But when he arrived at her door the old woman looked at him with troubled eyes.

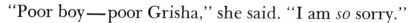

"Poor boy—poor Grisha," she said. "I am *so* sorry."

"What are you sorry about?" asked Grisha.

"Your goat, Grisha! Your goat is no more!"

"My goat is no more!" Grisha was shocked. *"But what happened?"*

"One day the goat was eating grass in the field when I saw a shadow on the ground," Olga explained. The shadow came fast—*very* fast. It was a chicken-hawk. And in just a few minutes—you wouldn't believe it!—before I knew what was happening the hawk picked up your goat and carried it away! I am *so* sorry, Grisha!"

"But chicken-hawks don't eat goats!" Grisha exclaimed. "A hawk couldn't even pick one up!"

"This one did," said Fat Olga.

As they talked a small crowd of neighbors gathered around them. They looked angry but they held their tongues until Grisha spoke.

"What will I do?" he cried. "I need milk. I have no food and no money and now I have no goat either! Please lend me your cow until I can buy another goat."

28

"Certainly not!" said Fat Olga.

"But the boy will go hungry!" said one neighbor.

"He will starve," shouted another.

"You *must* at least lend the cow to him," said still another.

Olga did not like the sound of anger in her neighbors' voices so she said as sweetly as possible, "Yes, my dear Grisha, for a week you may have the cow. And then you must bring her back to me."

One week later Grisha was strolling through the marketplace when Fat Olga caught sight of him. Rushing toward him she shouted, "Grisha! Grisha! The week is up! I want my cow back!"

"Oh, I am *so* sorry," Grisha said. "I took very good care of her. I milked her and fed her and one evening I took her down to the river for a drink. And *then* it happened."

"*What* happened?" cried Fat Olga with alarm.

"A huge fish jumped right out of the river and pulled the cow in with her. There was nothing I could do. But I am terribly sorry."

30

"Oh! Oh! Oh! What a thief!" Olga shouted. People came to see what was the matter.

"I want my cow back *right now!*" Olga screamed. And taking Grisha by the ear she rushed to the chief policeman. The chief policeman took Grisha and Olga to the mayor. When she told him what had happened he said sternly, "I never heard of a fish that could pull a cow into the river! How can such a thing be possible, Grisha?"

"That's what *I* wondered when Olga told me about the chicken-hawk that carried my goat into the sky when I left her with Olga!" Grisha said.

"Olga told you that?" questioned the mayor.

"Yes, sir," Grisha replied, "and I need my goat very much."

33

The mayor smiled to himself as if to say, "*Now* I see what has happened!" He thought for a long time and then said, "What you have both told me is miraculous indeed. Yes, the world is full of miracles! And I predict that two others are about to take place. In fact, I am convinced that tomorrow Grisha will find his goat in front of his house and Olga will find her cow in front of hers! If these miracles do not happen I assure you that I will find some way to *make* them happen!"

Just as the mayor predicted, the goat and the cow did appear. Fat Olga was so angry that she tripped as she brought the milk in from the barn. But Grisha smiled with pleasure as he tasted the warm fresh milk from his goat.

*The tale of a boy who knows
the value of a simple life.*

FISHING ALL DAY

Nikki loved nothing more than fishing in the river on a sunny day. He loved to watch the shining blue water. He loved the cool river bank. But most of all he loved to take his aunt a heavy basket of fine fresh fish at the end of the afternoon. Nikki's mother had died years ago.

One day in the beginning of summer Nikki became friends with Simon Smulin who had rented a big house in the neighborhood. A rich merchant from Moscow, Simon and his wife had everything they wanted except children. As the lovely summer days passed they grew more and more fond of Nikki.

Every afternoon Simon and his wife came down to the river to fish on the same river bank with their young friend. They ate and talked and watched with amazement as—every day—Nikki went home with a basket of fish.

"What a nice young boy!" Simon said to his wife.

"Look how clever he is at catching fish," she agreed.

"He could do other things if he wanted," Simon said. "He is the kind of boy who could do anything well."

"Yes, the boy is *very* clever," said Mrs. Smulin.

"A joy!" her husband exclaimed.

By the time summer drew to a close Simon Smulin and his wife liked Nikki very much. When they were about to leave for Moscow Simon said, "My young friend, the summer is over and we must go home. As you know, we have no children. We would like to take you with us and have you live at our home."

40

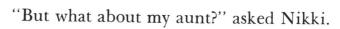

"But what about my aunt?" asked Nikki.

"Don't worry! We'll fix that," said Simon.

"Well, I would like to visit Moscow," Nikki said.

"Oh no," exclaimed Simon, "not to visit but to *live* with us all the time."

"But what would I do?" asked Nikki.

"You would go to school," said Simon.

"And a very good school!" his wife added.

"And then what?" asked Nikki.

"Well . . ." Simon thought, "then I would give you a job in my business."

"And what would I do there?" Nikki asked.

U.S. 1767649

"Why, you would start at the bottom, my boy, just as I did!" Simon said. "You'd learn everything there is to learn in the mail room and the shipping room. You'd become a foreman and then a department head. You'd learn about selling and accounting and eventually you would become a general manager!"

"And then——?"

"Well," said Simon, "when I die you would have *everything*. You would inherit the entire business! You would have my house, my paintings and all of my possessions."

"And *then* what?" questioned Nikki.

44

"Why . . . you would be one of the richest men in Moscow!" Simon said. "You could do anything in the world that you want. You could come up here and fish all day if you want."

Nikki put another worm on his fish hook and looked back at the beautiful quiet river. "I'm doing that right now!" he said.

47